The Three Little SUPERPIGS

ONCE UPON A TIME

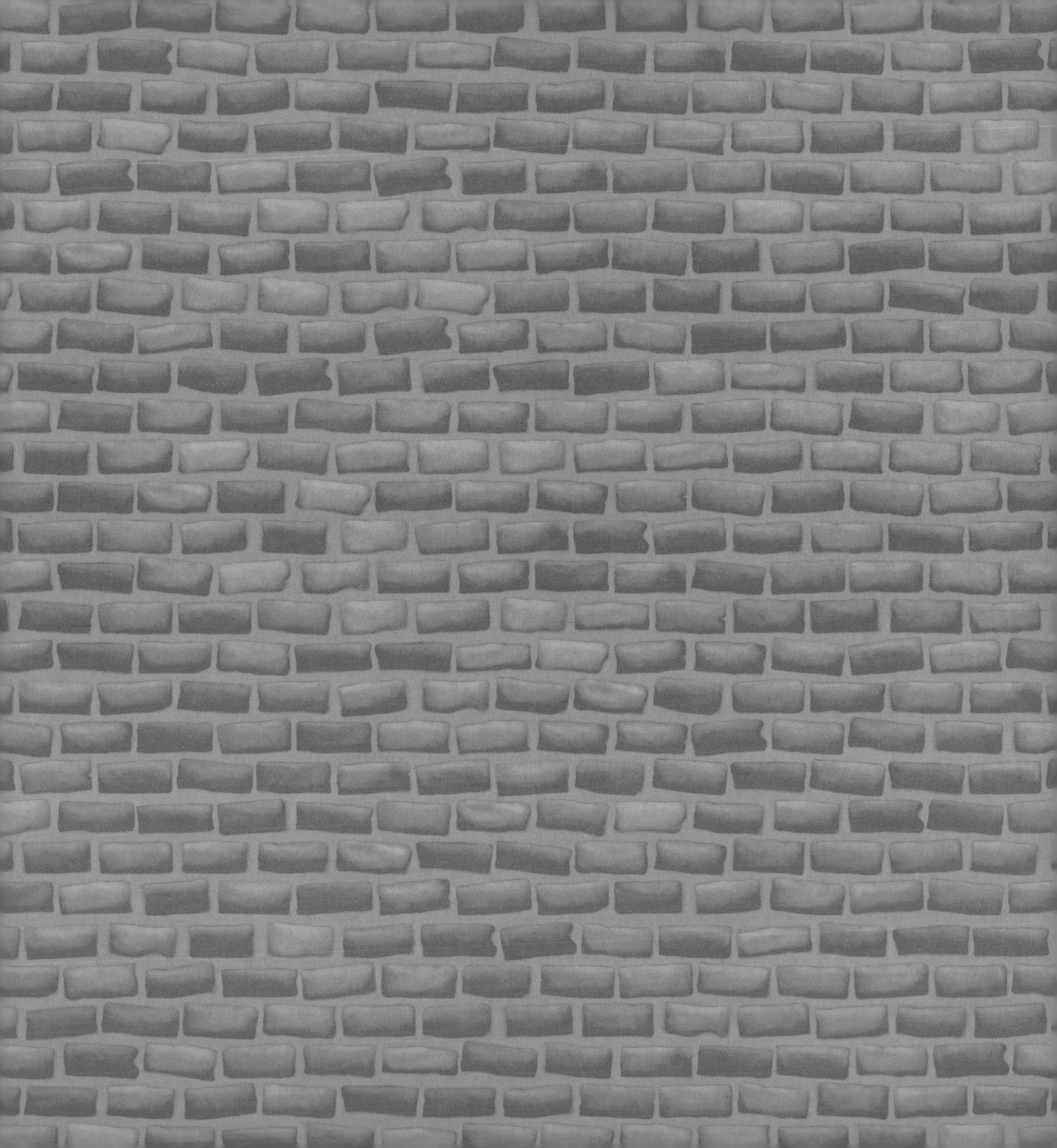

For my gorgeous Lucy and Amy x

The Three Little Superpigs: Once Upon a Time was originally published in the United Kingdom
by Fourth Wall Publishing in 2017 under the title *The Three Little Superpigs: The Origin.*

ISBN 978-1-338-53224-1

10 9 8 7 6 5 4 3 2 1   19 20 21 22 23

Printed in the U.S.A. 141

This edition first printing 2019

The Three Little SUPERPIGS

ONCE UPON A TIME

Written and illustrated by
Claire Evans

Scholastic Inc.

Once upon a time,
there were
three little pigs.

They dreamed
of becoming
SUPERHEROES!

In fact, they were so obsessed that their family house became cluttered with all of their superhero collections.

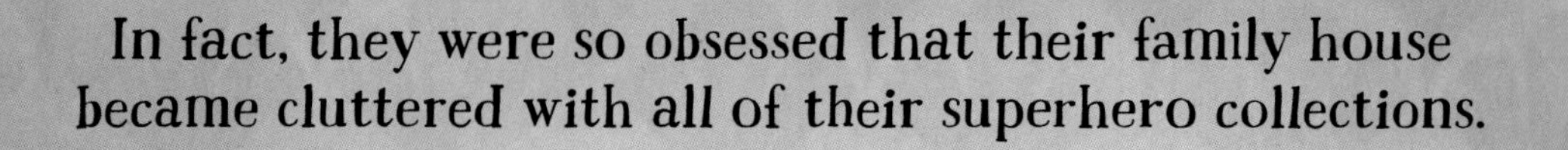

So one day, Mother Pig told her *little* superheroes
it was time to find their own homes,
and she waved good-bye.

They walked for hours,
crossing dangerous rivers
and climbing steep cliffs . . .

. . . until finally, they arrived at their destination –

Fairyland.

After an exhausting trip, the pigs decided to set up camp for the night and build their new homes in the morning.

Welcome to
FAIRYLAND

While toasting marshmallows in their superhero costumes,
the pigs met a new friend – Little Red Riding Hood.
She warned them about the Big Bad Wolf,
who'd been terrorizing Fairyland.

The Wolf had kidnapped
Mary's little lamb . . .

. . . and stolen sheep's clothing!

He'd even been disguising himself
as different grandmas and stolen *their* clothing!
The pigs were warned to be on their guard.

The next morning, two of the pigs were desperate to play superheroes with their new friends, so they built their houses as quickly as possible!

The first little pig chose straw to build his house, and he gathered all he could find.

The second little pig chose to build his house out of sticks, and he collected them from high and low.

And in no time at all,
their new homes were ready.

While his two brothers were having fun, the third little pig was patiently building his house out of bricks.

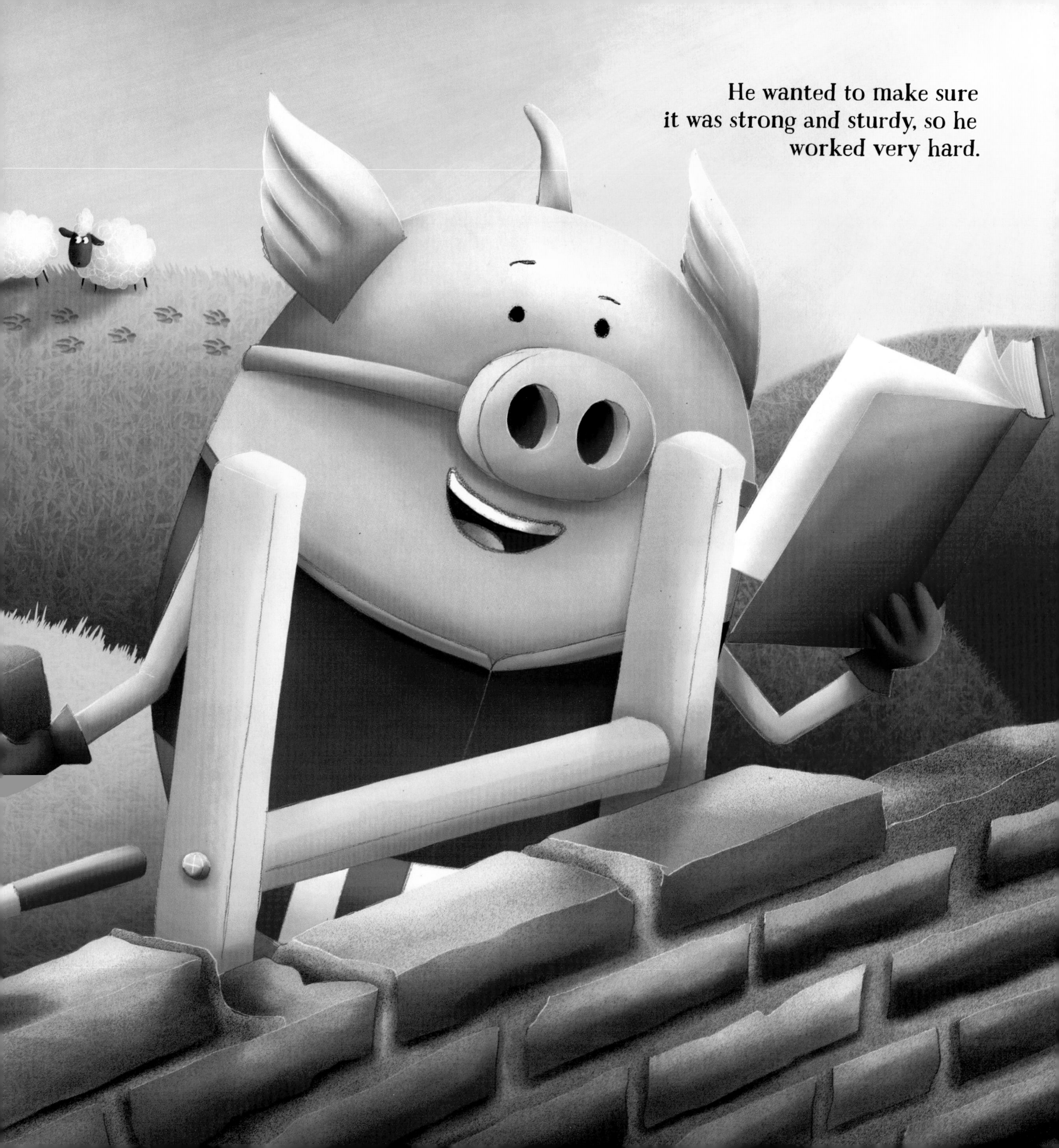

He wanted to make sure
it was strong and sturdy, so he
worked very hard.

DANGER!!
WOLF
ROAMS
HERE!!!

Finally, all three houses were ready and the pigs were very happy in their new homes.

Suddenly,
the first little pig
was startled by a
terrible growl outside
his window.
It was the BIG BAD WOLF!

"Little pig, little pig,
let me come in!"
he cried.

"Not by the hair
on my chinny
chin chin!"
squealed the panicked pig.

"Then I'll HUFF,
and I'll PUFF, and I'll blow your house in!"
growled the Wolf.

WHOOOSSSHH!

And with one puff,

he blew the house in!

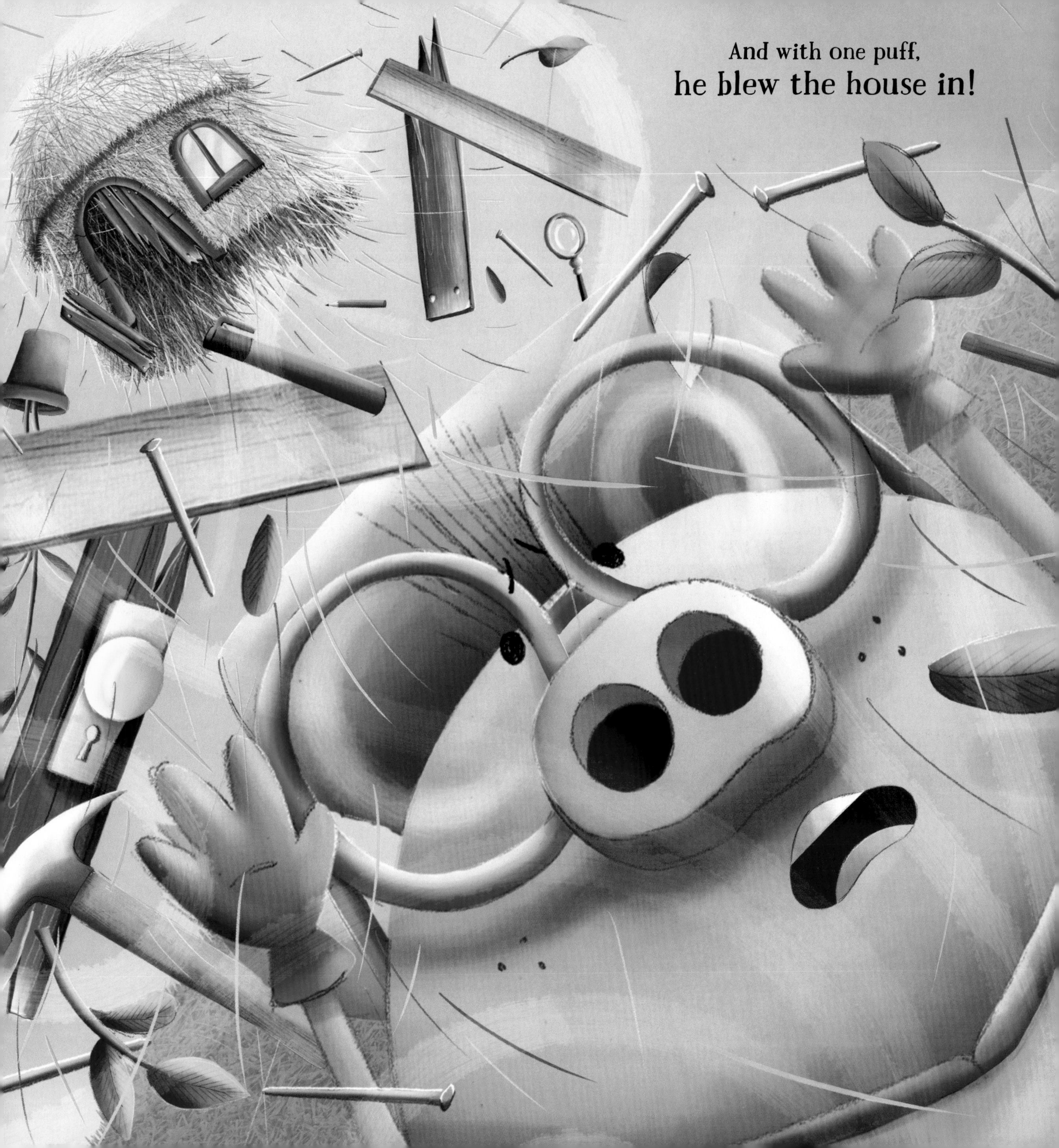

The first little pig ran for cover to
his brother's house of sticks.

"Little pigs, little pigs, let me come in!"

bellowed the Wolf.

"Not by the hairs on our chinny chin chins!" cried the pigs.

"Then I'll HUFF,
and I'll PUFF,
and I'll BLOW
YOUR HOUSE IN!"

So he huffed,
and he puffed, and . . .

...WHOOOOSSSHHHH!

He blew the stick house in!

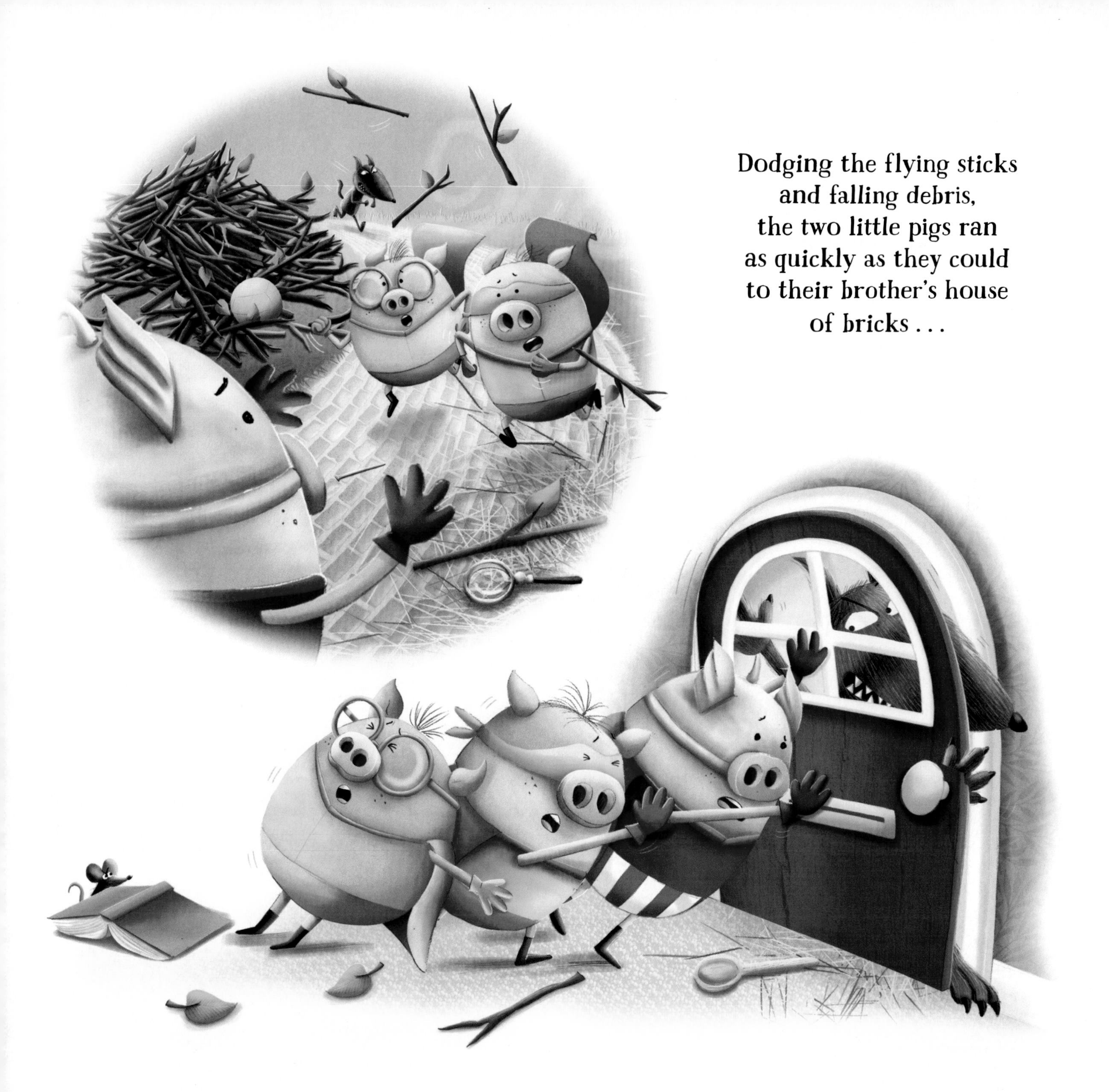

Dodging the flying sticks
and falling debris,
the two little pigs ran
as quickly as they could
to their brother's house
of bricks . . .

. . . narrowly escaping the nasty Wolf, who was getting very angry – and very hungry!

"Little pigs, little pigs, let me come in!" demanded the Wolf.

"Not by the hairs on our chinny chin chins!" the pigs replied.

"Then I'll **huff**, and I'll **puff**, and I'll **blow your house in!**" screamed the Wolf.

So he HUFFED,
and he PUFFED...

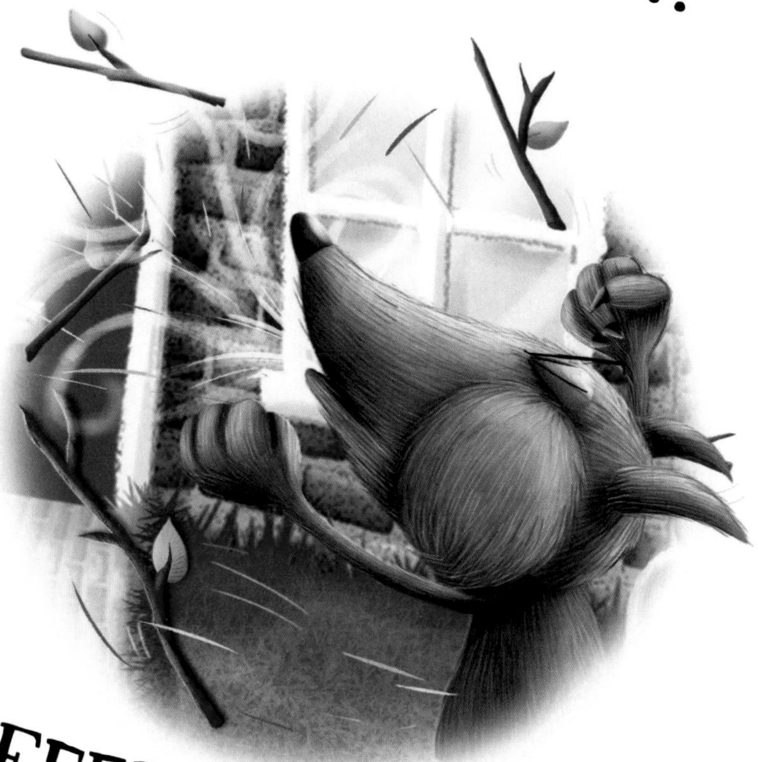

...and he HUFFED,
and he PUFFED...

but the brick house
would not blow in.

The Wolf
was furious!

Suddenly, the pigs were startled by a loud clanging noise from outside.
The cunning Big Bad Wolf had made another plan to climb onto the roof and sneak down the chimney!

Two of the pigs started to panic,
but the third little pig had a super plan.
He had been boiling a pan of water
on the fire all along!

HOW TO
BOIL A
WOLF

So as the Wolf came
hurtling down the chimney,
he fell bottom-first into
the bubbling, hot pan!

With a piercing shriek, he jumped out of the water, and straight into the pigs' net! The Big Bad Wolf was defeated!

The pigs waved good-bye to the silly old Wolf as he was carted off to prison.

With Fairyland safe at last, the pigs' dreams of becoming real superheroes had finally come true, as the whole town cheered their special new name . . .

"Hooray for the THREE LITTLE SUPERPIGS!"

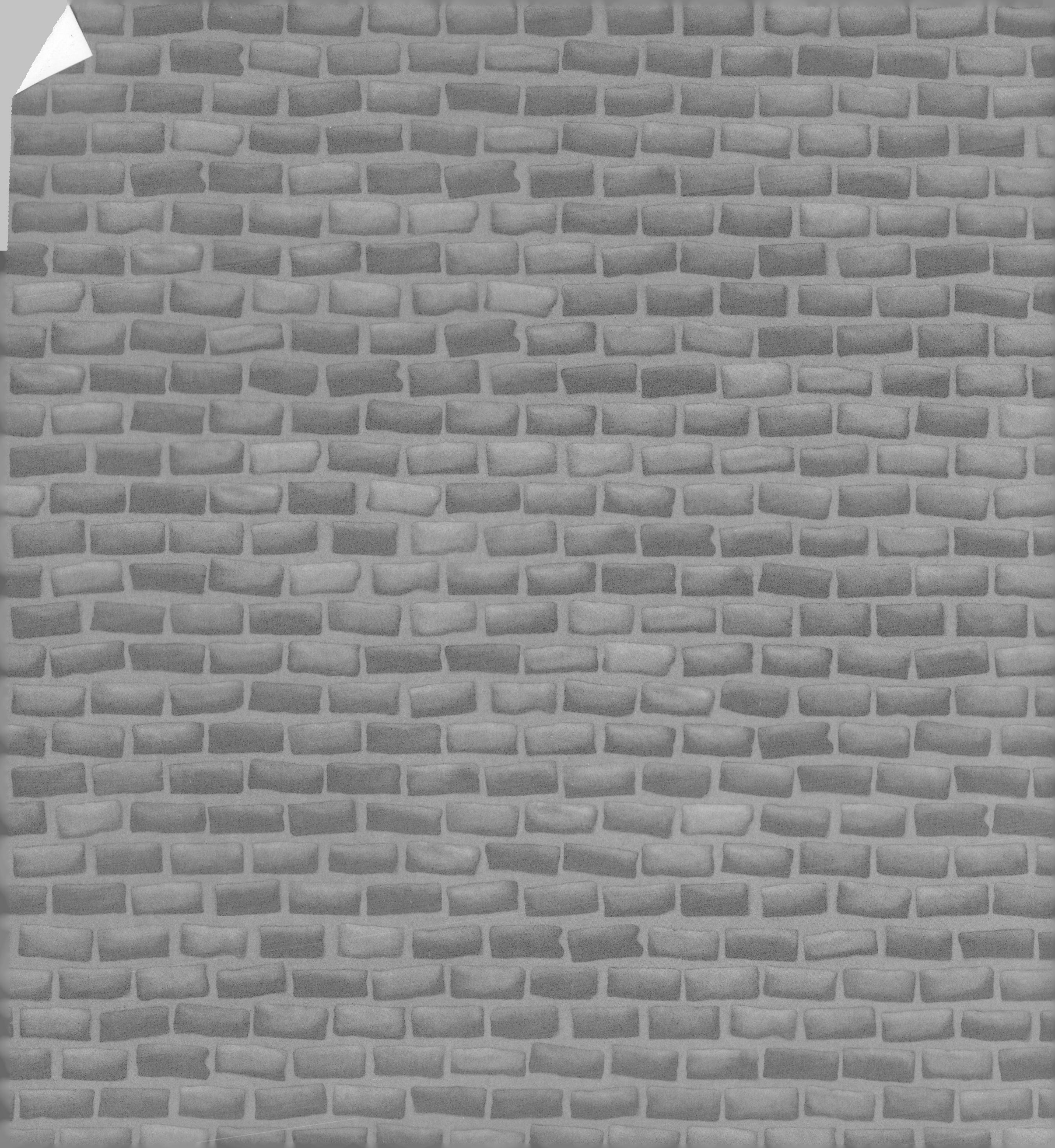